For Hazel Basil, I love you to the universe times infinity.
—B. H.

For Emmi, the coolest kid I know.
—A. S.

Text copyright © 2023 Brooke Hartman
Illustrations copyright © 2023 Anna Süßbauer

First published in 2023 by Page Street Kids
an imprint of
Page Street Publishing Co.
27 Congress Street, Suite 1511
Salem, MA 01970
www.pagestreetpublishing.com

Distributed by Macmillan, sales in Canada by The Canadian Manda Group
23 24 25 26 27 CCO 5 4 3 2 1
ISBN-13: 978-1-64567-628-7
ISBN-10: 1-64567-628-5

CIP data for this book is available from the Library of Congress.

This book was typeset in Brocha.
The illustrations were created digitally.
Cover and book design by Julia Tyler for Page Street Kids.
Edited by Kayla Tostevin for Page Street Kids.

Printed and bound in Shenzhen, Guangdong, China

Page Street Publishing uses only materials from suppliers who are committed to responsible
and sustainable forest management.

Page Street Publishing protects our planet by donating to nonprofits like The Trustees,
which focuses on local land conservation.

WATCH OUT FOR THE LION!

Brooke Hartman

illustrated by **Anna Süßbauer**

STOP RIGHT WHERE YOU ARE!

PAGE STREET KiDS

DO NOT GO ANY FARTHER.

I'm warning you,
somewhere very close,
there's a growling, prowling
LION!

SNOUT

FANGS

HOW TO SPOT A LION

TAIL

EARS

CLAWS

With a brushy, bristly tail, clashing, curvy claws,
two twitchy ears, ferocious, fearsome fangs,
and a snuffly, snarly—

UH-OH.
WHAT'S THAT?

Is it the . . .

LION!

That's the king of the jungle, I tell you!
Just look at that **brushy, bristly tail.**
Actually, don't look.
Cover your eyes and maybe it will go away.

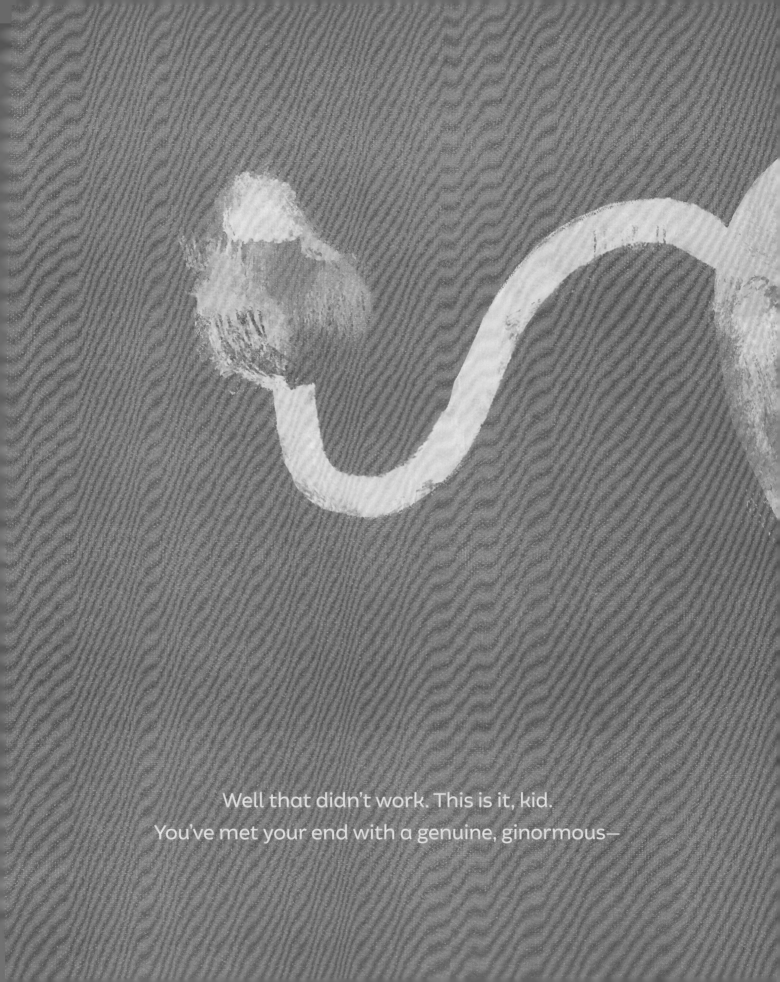

Well that didn't work. This is it, kid.
You've met your end with a genuine, ginormous—

GIRAFFE?

Wow, that giraffe is really tall.
You'd have to stand on your tiptoes just to reach its back!
Speaking of which, you should turn around
and tiptoe right back out of here.
Because somewhere super-duper close, there truly is a . . .

LION!

See those **curvy claws?**
You can almost feel how pointy they are!
Wait, I don't actually mean feel them.
Those are the **claws of destruction.**
You **do not touch** the claws of destruction!
I said don't . . .

YOU TOUCHED THEM!

That's it. You've done it now.
Invoked the wrath of a savage, salivating . . .

SLOTH?

Don't look at me like that.
Of course I know a sloth isn't a lion.
Did you know a sloth isn't a lion?
You did? Oh. That's fascinating.
Know what's not so fascinating?
What will happen if you keep going.
Because if you do, you'll soon be running away,
screaming your lungs out.

You might as well practice your scream now.
Try it with me:

Aaaaiiiieee!

Let's do that again, this time with more of that
"I'm about to be eaten alive" feeling. Ready?

EiiiiAAAAA!

Ssshhh!

Be very quiet. See those **twitchy ears?**
Lions have exceptional hearing.
They can detect prey from over a mile off.

There's no escape now. I can't even watch.

Tell me when it's over.

Never mind. You won't be here to tell me when it's over.

Because that is one hundred percent a horrible, hairy—

HAMSTER.

Well, this is embarrassing.

Listen, I admit I might've made a few minor errors before.
But I'm begging you, please, please,
please don't go any farther.
Because if you do, you're going to find yourself
face-to-face with a . . .

LION!

No denying it this time.
Just look at those **ferocious fangs!**
Know what those teeth are good for? Eating meat!
And guess who's made of meat?
You got it.

You're really in a pickle now, kid.
I hope you like snacks, because you're about to be one.
Lion lunch. A child cheeseburger. Rugrat ravioli.
Better hold on to your biscuits, because those are the
carnivorous canines of a wicked, wild—

WALRUS.

All right. I give up.
There isn't a lion within miles of here. Not one.
Don't even try to tell me otherwise.

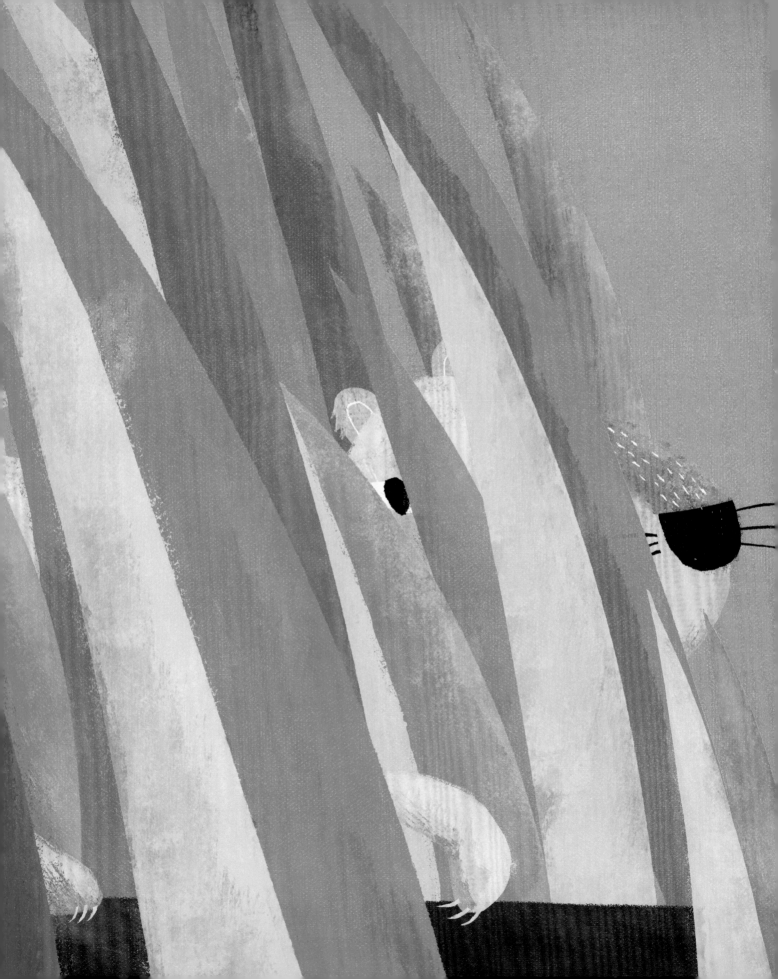

Oh, I see you **snuffly snout.**
Whatever you are, you can come out now.
You're probably an alpaca. Or a wombat, for all I know.

With a **brushy, bristly tail**...
clashing, curvy claws...
two twitchy ears...
and ferocious (gulp)... fearsome...

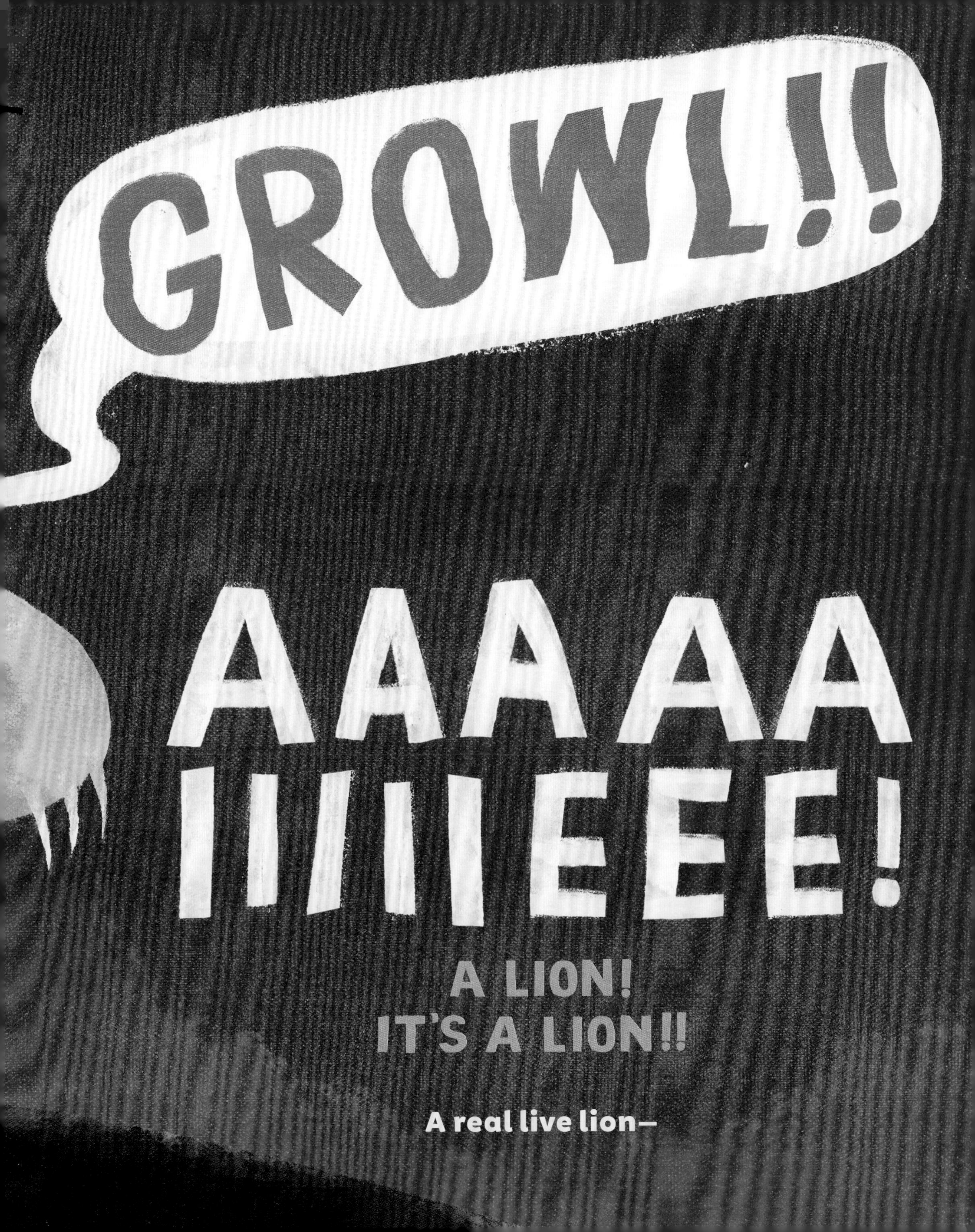

A LION!
IT'S A LION!!

A real live lion—

CUB.

That is actually quite adorable.

See? I told you there was a lion.
Maybe next time you'll believe me.

Because you never know what
could be lurking around the corner.